A Bear for Christmas

by HOLLY KELLER

GREENWILLOW BOOKS
New York

JE
cop. IV

Library of Congress Cataloging in Publication Data

Keller, Holly.   A bear for Christmas.
Summary: Joey sneaks his Christmas present, a toy bear, out of its box before Christmas and is upset when he accidentally rips it.
[1. Gifts—Fiction.   2. Christmas—Fiction.   I. Title.

PZ7.K28132Be   1986   [E]   85-12645
ISBN 0-688-05988-0   ISBN 0-688-05989-9 (lib. bdg.)

The three-color preseparated art was prepared as a black pen-and-ink drawing with halftone overlays for yellow, red, and gray. The typeface is Korinna.

FOR RANDY

Joey looked at the big package on the table.
It was from Grandma.

The brown paper was torn and Joey could
see the shiny red box underneath.
He knew it was for Christmas.

At lunchtime the package was gone.
"Where's the big box?" Joey asked Mama.
"Drink your milk," Mama said,
and Joey knew it was for him.

Joey thought about the package
all afternoon.
At night he couldn't sleep.

In the morning Joey waited until
Mama was busy in the kitchen.
He just wanted to see it one more time.

He looked in the cellar and in the closets.

He looked behind the curtains and under the beds.

Then he went up to the attic
and there it was.

First he lifted the lid just a crack,
then all the way.

The bear was almost as big as Joey.
Joey thought he would name him Fred, like
the man in the grocery who gave him pretzels.

When Arnold came over to play,
Joey told him about Fred.
"Do you want to see?" Joey whispered.

"Wow," Arnold said. "He's big. Can we take him out?"
 Joey wasn't sure.
"Just for a minute," Arnold pleaded.

"I think we should put him back," Joey said.

"Let's just play with him a little," Arnold said.

"No," Joey insisted. "We better not."

Joey reached for Fred
and Arnold pulled back.

"Let go," Joey shouted. "He's mine."
"I'll tell on you," Arnold shouted back.

Joey heard the rip, but he couldn't look.

"Gosh," Arnold said. "I didn't mean it, Joey."
Joey put Fred back in the box.
Arnold wanted to go home.

That night Mama made spaghetti
for dinner, but Joey couldn't eat.
"I'm full," he said.

Joey lay down on the sofa and
fell asleep in his clothes.
He dreamed about running away.

Papa bought a Christmas tree and Mama
made a big bowl of popcorn for stringing.
"You do it," Joey said.

And he did not want to sing Christmas carols.

On Christmas morning Joey got some books,
a drum, a boat for his bath, and a little train.

The big red box was right behind the tree.
"Don't you want that one?" Papa asked.

Mama opened the box. Joey could see Fred
under the tissue. "Mama…," Joey whispered,
but Mama was already lifting Fred out.

Joey blinked. Mama smiled.
"Merry Christmas, Joey," she said.
"I think he's better now."

cop.l

"How did you know?" Joey asked.

Mama laughed. "I peeked, too," she said.

"His name is Fred," Joey told Papa.

"That's a fine name," Papa said.

"Who is hungry?" Mama asked.

"Everybody," Joey practically shouted.

"Good," Mama said. "Let's have some breakfast."